Books by James Howe

Bunnicula Books
Bunnicula (with Deborah Howe)
Howliday Inn
The Celery Stalks at Midnight
Nighty-Nightmare
Return to Howliday Inn
Bunnicula Strikes Again!
Bunnicula Meets Edgar Allan Crow

Bunnicula and Friends
The Vampire Bunny
Hot Fudge
Scared Silly
Rabbit-cadabra!
The Fright Before Christmas
Creepy-Crawly Birthday

Tales from the House of Bunnicula
It Came from Beneath the Bed!
Invasion of the Mind Swappers from Asteroid 6!
Howie Monroe and the Doghouse of Doom
Screaming Mummies of the Pharoah's Tomb II
Bud Barkin, Private Eye
The ~~Amazing~~ Odorous Adventures of Stinky Dog

The Misfits Series
The Misfits
Totally Joe
Addie on the Inside
Also Known as Elvis

Novels
A Night Without Stars

Morgan's Zoo
The Watcher

Sebastian Barth Mysteries
What Eric Knew
Stage Fright
Eat Your Poison, Dear
Dew Drop Dead

Pinky and Rex Series
Pinky and Rex
Pinky and Rex Get Married
Pinky and Rex and the Mean Old Witch
Pinky and Rex and the Spelling Bee
Pinky and Rex Go to Camp
Pinky and Rex and the New Baby
Pinky and Rex and the Double-Dad Weekend
Pinky and Rex and the Bully
Pinky and Rex and the New Neighbors
Pinky and Rex and the Perfect Pumpkin
Pinky and Rex and the School Play
Pinky and Rex and the Just-Right Pet

Picture Books
There's a Monster Under My Bed
There's a Dragon in My Sleeping Bag
Teddy Bear's Scrapbook (with Deborah Howe)
Horace and Morris but mostly Dolores
Horace and Morris Join the Chorus (but what about Dolores?)
Horace and Morris Say Cheese (which makes Dolores sneeze!)

Edited by James Howe
The Color of Absence: 12 Stories about Loss and Hope
*13: Thirteen Stories That Capture the Agony and Ecstasy of
    Being Thirteen*

BUNNICULA

A Rabbit-Tale of Mystery

40th Anniversary Edition

BY DEBORAH AND JAMES HOWE

Illustrated by Alan Daniel

Atheneum Books for Young Readers

NEW YORK   LONDON   TORONTO   SYDNEY   NEW DELHI

To Mildred and Lester Smith
—*with love*

atheneum

Atheneum Books for Young Readers
An imprint of Simon & Schuster Children's Publishing Division
1230 Avenue of the Americas, New York, New York 10020

For information about special discounts for bulk purchases, please contact
Simon & Schuster Special Sales at 1-866-506-1949 or business@simonandschuster.com.
The Simon & Schuster Speakers Bureau can bring authors to your live event.
For more information or to book an event, contact the Simon & Schuster Speakers
Bureau at 1-866-248-3049 or visit our website at www.simonspeakers.com.
Also available in an Atheneum Books for Young Readers hardcover edition
Book design by Mike Rosamilia
The text for this book was set in Stempel Garamond.
The illustrations for this book were rendered in pen and ink.
Manufactured in China
0319 SCP
This Atheneum Books for Young Readers paperback edition May 2019
10 9 8 7 6 5 4 3 2 1
CIP data for this book is available from the Library of Congress.
ISBN 978-1-5344-3593-3 (pbk)
ISBN 978-1-4391-3205-0 (eBook)

Bunnicula 40th Anniversary Edition
is in memory of Deborah Howe.

Contents

INTRODUCTION TO THE 40th ANNIVERSARY EDITION OF *BUNNICULA*

by James Howe

Bunnicula began not from words but from pictures. Moving pictures. To be exact, *Bunnicula* got its start from watching too many vampire movies late at night. I guess I should say too many *bad* vampire movies.

Back in 1977, television had five channels, and movies were shown on and off throughout the day and into the night. Night was when the vampire movies came on. My wife, Debbie, and I, both underemployed actors with lots of time on our hands, stayed up many a night watching movies because (a) we didn't have anywhere we needed to be in the morning, (b) we loved movies, and (c) we loved vampires. Not that vampires are especially lovable.

After watching one too many bad—which is to say, silly—vampire movies, I turned to Debbie and asked, "What if I wanted to make the worst vampire movie ever? Or at least the silliest? What's the least likely vampire you can imagine?"

Before she could answer, I burst out: "A bunny!"

And there it was.

But I didn't make a movie. And although I loved to write, I did so only for pleasure and not ever with the thought that I could actually write an entire book. No, at first, Bunnicula was just a character who lived in my head. I was an actor, remember. I was used to having characters living in my head. One day, I made a birthday card and drew my idea of what Bunnicula looked like.

(Which explains why, when Bunnicula did become a book, someone else drew the pictures!)

It was Debbie's mother's idea that we write a book about him. So we sat down one night after dinner, notebook in hand, and gave it a try.

Debbie and I spent close to a year writing *Bunnicula*. About midway through the writing we learned that Debbie had cancer and that she had only months to live. We let the writing go for a time, then returned to it because we needed to laugh. After her death in June 1978, I didn't think about getting the book published or writing another book. I was just trying to get through the days.

I was working as an assistant to a literary agent (something had to pay the rent, and acting wasn't doing it), and it was my boss who suggested an editor who might be interested in publishing the children's book Debbie and I had written just for our own amusement. That editor didn't think it was right for her publishing company and suggested an editor at Atheneum Publishers.

I sent the book off and nervously waited for two weeks to hear back.

Jean Karl called me on a Monday morning and said, "I just got back from a two-week vacation. I found your manuscript on my desk this morning. I sat down immediately and read it. I love it. I want to publish it."

Three days later, a four-page contract arrived in the mail, which I signed and returned.

If only getting published were always that easy!

A week later, I met Jean—who I would later learn was a legend among children's book editors—at Atheneum's headquarters on 42nd Street in New York City. When I was shown into her office, I found her seated at her desk, which was clean of everything but a phone, a manuscript she was in the middle of reading, and the pencil in her hand. She greeted me warmly, replaced the manuscript in front of her with mine, and said two things I will never forget:

(1) "We are delighted to be publishing your book. Now I want you to know that this is *your* book, and we want you to be happy with it. So you don't have to make any of the changes I'm going to suggest."

She then went through the manuscript with me and suggested a handful of small changes. I made every one.

And (2) "What do you have in mind for the illustrations?"

Well, Debbie and I had never given any thought to the illustrations. We were word people. And honestly, I hadn't expected to be consulted. But I always loved the drawings that illustrated my favorite book in the whole world. And that's what I said: "How about something like Garth Williams's illustrations in *Charlotte's Web*?"

I don't know if Alan Daniel's illustrations are like Garth Williams's or not, but I couldn't have been more pleased when I saw his version of Bunnicula and the other characters for the first time. I knew at once that these were the characters Debbie and I had created in words.

It has now been forty years since this image of Bunnicula first appeared. In celebration of the fortieth anniversary of the book's publication, my publisher and I have put together a gallery of just some of the many other visual interpretations of Bunnicula over the years. Just as I could not have imagined that this book, with its odd and humble origins, would launch my career as a children's author, I couldn't conceive of all the different ways it would be given new life: six sequels (illustrated by four different artists), spinoff series (with entirely new artists), foreign publications, stage plays and musicals, a TV special, a cartoon series, and coming soon: a graphic novel adaptation.

All of these different takes on *Bunnicula* have meant different visual interpretations as well. In our gallery at the end of the book, we are focusing on the character of Bunnicula himself: not only those images created by professional illustrators and animators, but also puppet makers (for the stage versions), costume designers (including me: see my daughter Zoey's Halloween costume), and readers like you. I've received thousands of drawings by readers over the years and only wish I could have included more here. Maybe you'll be inspired to try your hand at drawing your own version of Bunnicula.

There's much more on my website (jameshowe. com) about the writing of *Bunnicula* and all that's happened since. But don't go there yet. First, enjoy reading—or rereading—the original story. Have fun looking at Alan Daniel's first-ever drawings of Bunnicula, Harold, Chester, and the Monroes. And then, as the TV cartoon Harold might say, *prepare to have your mind blown* by all the ways Bunnicula has appeared in the past forty years!

BUNNICULA
40th Anniversary Edition

EDITOR'S NOTE

The book you are about to read was brought to my attention in a most unusual way. One Friday afternoon, just before closing time, I heard a scratching sound at the front door of my office. When I opened the door, there before me stood a sad-eyed, droopy-eared dog carrying a large, plain envelope in his mouth. He dropped it at my feet, gave me a soulful glance and with great, quiet dignity sauntered away.

Inside the envelope was the manuscript of the book you now hold in your hands, together with this letter:

Gentlemen:

The enclosed story is true. It happened in this very town, to me and the family with whom I reside. I have changed the names of the family in order to protect them, but in all other respects, everything you will read here is factual.

Allow me to introduce myself. My name is Harold. I come to writing purely by chance. My full-time occupation is dog. I live with Mr. and Mrs. X (called here the "Monroes") and their two sons: Toby, age eight, and Pete, age ten. Also sharing our home is a cat named Chester, whom I am pleased to call my friend. We were a typical American family—and still are, though the events related in my story have, of course, had their effect on our lives.

I hope you will find this tale of sufficient interest to yourself and your readers to warrant its publication.

Sincerely,
Harold X

One
THE ARRIVAL

I shall never forget the first time I laid these now tired old eyes on our visitor. I had been left home by the family with the admonition to take care of the house until they returned. That's something they always say to me when they go out: "Take care of the house, Harold. You're the watchdog." I think it's their way of making up for not taking me with them. As if I *wanted* to go anyway. You can't lie down at the movies and still see the screen. And people think you're being impolite if you fall asleep and start to snore, or scratch yourself in public. No thank you, I'd rather be stretched out on my favorite rug in front of a nice, whistling radiator.

But I digress. I was talking about that first night. Well, it was cold, the rain was pelting the windows, the wind was howling, and it felt pretty good to be indoors. I was lying on the rug with my head on my paws just staring absently at the front door. My friend Chester was curled up on the brown velvet armchair, which years ago he'd staked out as his own. I saw that once again he'd covered the whole seat with his cat hair, and I chuckled to myself, picturing the scene tomorrow. (Next to grasshoppers, there is nothing that frightens Chester more than the vacuum cleaner.)

In the midst of this reverie, I heard a car pull into the driveway. I didn't even bother to get up and see who it was. I knew it had to be my family—the Monroes—since it was just about time for the movie to be over. After a moment, the front door flew open. There they stood in the doorway: Toby and Pete and Mom and Dad Monroe. There was a flash of lightning, and in its glare I noticed that Mr. Monroe was carrying a little bundle—a bundle with tiny glistening eyes.

Pete and Toby bounded into the room, both talking at the top of their lungs. Toby shouted, "Put him over here, Dad."

"Take your boots off. You're soaking wet," replied his mother, somewhat calmly I thought, under the circumstances.

"But Mom, what about the—"

"First, stop dripping on the carpet."

"Would somebody like to take this?" asked Mr. Monroe, indicating the bundle with the eyes. "I'd like to remove my coat."

"I will," Pete yelled.

"No, I will," said Toby. "I found him."

"You'll drop him."

"I will not."

"You will, too."

"Mom, Pete punched me!"

"*I'll* take him," said Mrs. Monroe. "Take off your coats this minute!" But she became so involved in helping the boys out of their coats that she didn't take him at all.

My tranquil evening had been destroyed and no one had even said hello to me. I whimpered to remind them that I was there.

"Harold!" cried Toby. "Guess what happened to me." And then, all over again, everyone started talking at once.

At this point, I feel I must explain something. In

our family, everyone treats everyone else with great respect for his or her intelligence. That goes for the animals as well as the people. Everything that happens to them is explained to us. It's never been just "Good boy, Harold," or "Use the litter box, Chester" at our house. Oh no, with us it's "Hey Harold, Dad got a raise and now we're in a higher tax bracket," or "Come sit on the bed, Chester, and watch this *Wild Kingdom* show. Maybe you'll see a relative." Which shows just how thoughtful they are. But after all, Mr. Monroe *is* a college professor and Mrs. Monroe *is* a lawyer, so we think of it as a rather special household. And we are, therefore, rather special pets. So it wasn't at all surprising to me that they took the time to explain the strange circumstances surrounding the arrival of the little bundle with the glistening eyes now among us.

It seems that they had arrived at the theater late, and rather than trip over the feet of the audience already seated, they decided to sit in the last row, which was empty. They tiptoed in and sat down very quietly, so they wouldn't disturb anyone. Suddenly, Toby, who's the little one, sprang up from his chair and squealed that he had sat on something. Mr. Monroe told him to stop making a fuss and move to another seat, but in an unusual display of independence, Toby said he wanted to see just what it was he had sat on. An usher came over to their row to shush them, and Mr. Monroe borrowed his flashlight. What they found on Toby's chair was the little blanketed bundle that was now sitting on Mr. Monroe's lap.

They now unwrapped the blanket, and there in the center was a tiny black and white rabbit, sitting in a shoebox filled with dirt. A piece of paper had been tied to his neck with a ribbon. There were words on the paper, but the Monroes were unable to decipher them because they were in a totally unfamiliar language. I moved closer for a better look.

Now, most people might call me a mongrel, but I have some pretty fancy bloodlines running through these veins and Russian wolfhound happens to be one of them. Because my family got around a lot, I was able to recognize the language as an obscure dialect of the Carpathian Mountain region. Roughly translated, it read, "Take good care of my baby." But I couldn't tell if it was a note from a bereaved mother or a piece of Roumanian sheet music.

The little guy was shivering from fear and cold. It was decided that Mr. Monroe and the boys would make a house for him out of an old crate and some heavy-duty wire mesh from the garage. For the night, the boys would make a bed for him in the shoebox. Toby and Pete ran outside to find the crate, and Mrs. Monroe went to the kitchen to get him some milk and lettuce. Mr. Monroe sat down, a dazed expression in his eyes, as if he were wondering how he came to be sitting in his own living room in a wet raincoat with a strange bunny on his lap.

I signaled to Chester and the two of us casually moseyed over to a corner of the room. We looked at each other.

"Well, what do you think?" I asked.

"I don't think rabbits like milk," he answered.

Chester and I were unable to continue our conversation because a deafening crash commanded our attention.

Pete yelled from the hallway: "Maaa! Toby broke the rabbit's house!"

"I didn't, I just dropped it. Pete won't let me carry it."

"It's too big. Toby's too little."

"I am not!"

"You are, too!"

"Okay, fellas," Mrs. Monroe called out as she entered with the milk and lettuce. "Let's try to get it in here with as little hysteria as possible, please."

Chester turned to me and said under his breath, "That lettuce looks repulsive, but if there's any milk left, *I* get it." I certainly wasn't going to argue with him. I'm a water man myself.

At that moment, the crate arrived, barely standing the strain of being pulled in two directions at once.

"Ma, Toby says he's going to keep the rabbit in his room. That's not fair. Harold sleeps in his room."

Only sometimes, I thought, when I know he's got a leftover ham sandwich in his drawer. Toby's a nice kid, don't get me wrong, but it doesn't hurt that he shares his stash with me. It was, after all, at one of those late night parties in Toby's room that I first developed my taste for chocolate cake. And Toby, noting my preference, has kept me in chocolate cake ever since. Pete, on the other hand, doesn't believe in sharing. And the only time I tried to sleep on his bed, he rolled over on me and pinned me by my ears so that I couldn't move for the rest of the night. I had a crick in my neck for days.

"But he's mine," Toby said. "I found him."

"You sat on him, you mean!"

"I found him, and he's sleeping in my room."

"You can keep smelly ol' Harold in your room, and Chester, too, if you want to, but I'm going to keep the rabbit in mine."

Smelly ol' Harold! I would have bitten his ankle, but I knew he hadn't changed his socks for a week. Smelly, indeed!

Mr. Monroe spoke up. "I think the best place for the rabbit is right here in the living room on that table by the window. It's light there, and he'll get lots of fresh air."

"Pete's taller than I am," Toby cried. "He'll be able to see the rabbit better."

"Too bad, squirt."

"Okay," said Mrs. Monroe through clenched teeth, "let's put him to bed and make him comfortable, and then we can all get some sleep."

"Why?" Pete asked. "I don't want to go to sleep."

Mrs. Monroe smiled a little too sweetly at Pete.

"Look, Ma," said Toby, "he's not drinking his milk."

Chester nudged me in the ribs. "Didn't I tell you?" he asked. "Excuse me while I make myself available."

"Hey," said Toby, "we gotta name him."

"Can't that wait until tomorrow?" asked Mr. Monroe.

The boys shouted in unison: "No! He has to have a name right now." I have to say I agreed with them. It took them three days to name me, and those were the three most anxious days of my life. I couldn't sleep at all, worrying that they were really going to call me Fluffy as Mrs. Monroe had suggested.

"Well, all right," sighed Mrs. Monroe, "what about . . . oh, say . . . Bun-Bun?"

Oh, oh. There she goes again, I thought. Where *does* she get them?

"Yech!" we all said.

"Well, then, how about Fluffy?" she offered hopefully.

Pete looked at his mother and smiled. "You never give up, do you, Ma?"

Meanwhile, Chester (who had also been named Fluffy for a short time) was rubbing against Mrs. Monroe's ankles and purring loudly.

"No, Chester, not now," she said, pushing him aside.

"He wants to help us name him, don't you Chester?" Toby asked, as he scooped him up into his arms. Chester shot me a look. I could tell this was not what he had in mind.

"Come on, Harold," Toby called, "you've got to help with the name, too."

I joined the family and serious thinking began. We all peered into the box. It was the first time I had really seen him. So, this is a rabbit, I thought. He sort of looks like Chester, only he's got longer ears and a shorter tail. And a motor in his nose.

"Well," said Pete, after a moment, "since we found him at the movies, why don't we call him Mr. Johnson?"

There was a moment of silence.

"Who's Mr. Johnson?" asked Toby.

"The guy who owns the movie theater," Pete answered.

No one seemed to like the idea.

"How about Prince?" said Mr. Monroe.

"Dad," said Toby, "are you kidding?"

"Well, I had a dog named Prince once," he replied lamely.

Prince, I thought, that's a silly name for a dog.

"We found him at a Dracula movie. Let's call him Dracula," Toby said.

"That's a stupid name," said Pete.

"No, it's not! And anyway, I found him, so I should get to name him."

"Mom, you're not going to let him name him, are you? That's favoritism, and I'll be traumatized if you do."

Mrs. Monroe looked in wonder at Pete.

"Please Mom, please Dad, let's name him Dracula," cried Toby, "please, please, please." And with each *please*, he squeezed Chester a little harder.

Mrs. Monroe picked up the bowl of milk and moved toward the kitchen. Chester followed her every movement with his eyes, which now seemed to be popping out of his head. When she reached the kitchen door, she turned back and said, "Let's not have any more arguments. We'll compromise. He's a bunny and we found him at a Dracula movie, so we'll call him Bunny-cula. Bun*ni*cula! That should make everybody happy, including me."

"What about me?" muttered Chester. "I won't be happy until she puts down that milk."

"Well, guys, is that okay with you?" she asked.

Toby and Pete looked at one another. And then at the rabbit. A smile grew on Toby's face.

"Yeah, Ma, I think that name is just right."

Pete shrugged. "It's okay. But I get to feed him."

"Okay, I'm going to put the milk back in the fridge. Maybe he'll drink it tomorrow."

"What about Chester?" Toby said, dropping the frantic cat to the floor. "Maybe he would like it." Chester made a beeline for Mrs. Monroe and looked up at her plaintively.

"Oh, Chester doesn't want any more milk, do you, Chester? You've already had your milk today." She reached down, patted Chester on his head, and walked into the kitchen. Chester didn't move.

"Okay, bedtime," said Mr. Monroe.

"Good night, Bunnicula," Toby said.

"Good night, Count Bunnicula," Pete said sarcastically, in what I took to be his attempt at a Transylvanian accent. I may be wrong but I thought I saw a flicker of movement from the cage.

"Good night, Harold. Good night, Chester." I licked Toby good night.

"Good night, smelly Harold. Good night, dumb Chester." I drooled on Pete's foot. "Mom, Harold drooled on my foot!"

"*Good night, Pete!*" Mrs. Monroe said with great finality as she came back into the living room, and then more calmly, "Good night, Harold. Good night, Chester."

Mr. and Mrs. Monroe went up the stairs together.

"You know, dear," Mr. Monroe said, "that was very clever. Bunnicula. I could never have thought of a name like that."

"Oh, I don't know, Robert." She smiled as she put her arm through his. "I think Prince is a lovely name, too."

The room was quiet. Chester was still sitting by the closed kitchen door in a state of shock. Slowly, he turned to me.

"I wish they *had* named him Fluffy," was all he said.

Two
MUSIC IN
THE NIGHT

I feel at this time there are a few things you should know about Chester. He is not your ordinary cat. (But then, I'm not your ordinary dog, since an ordinary dog wouldn't be writing this book, would he?)

Chester came into the house several years ago as a birthday gift for Mr. Monroe, along with two volumes of G. K. Chesterton (hence the name, Chester) and a first edition of Dickens' *A Tale of Two Cities.* As a result of this introduction to literature, and given the fact that Mr. Monroe is an English professor, Chester developed a taste of reading early in life. (I, on the other hand, have developed a taste for books. I found *Jonathan Livingston Seagull* particularly delicious.) From Chester's kittenhood on, Mr. Monroe has used him as a sounding board for all his student lectures. If Chester doesn't fall asleep when Mr. Monroe is talking, the lecture can be counted a success.

Every night when the family is sleeping, Chester goes to the bookshelf, selects his midnight reading, and curls up on his favorite chair. He especially likes mystery stories and tales of horror and the supernatural. As a result, he has developed a very vivid imagination.

I'm telling you this because I think it's important for you to know something of Chester's background before I relate to you the story of the events following the arrival of Bunnicula into our home. Let me begin with that first night.

It seems that after I went to sleep, Chester, still stewing over the lost milk, settled down with his latest book and attempted to ignore the rumbling in his stomach. The room was dark and quiet. This did not prevent his reading, of course, since as you know, cats can see in the dark. A shaft of moonlight fell across the rabbit's cage and spilled onto the floor below. The wind and rain had stopped and, as

Chester read Edgar Allan Poe's "The Fall of the House of Usher," he became increasingly aware of the eerie stillness that had taken their place. As Chester tells it, he suddenly felt compelled to look at the rabbit.

"I don't know what came over me," he said to me the next morning, "but a cold chill ran down my spine."

The little bunny had begun to move for the first time since he had been put in his cage. He lifted his tiny nose and inhaled deeply, as if gathering sustenance from the moonlight.

"He slicked his ears back close to his body, and for the first time," Chester said, "I noticed the peculiar marking on his forehead. What had seemed an ordinary black spot between his ears took on a strange v-shape, which connected with the big black patch that covered his back and each side of his neck. It looked as if he was wearing a coat . . . no, more like a *cape* than a coat."

Through the silence had drifted the strains of a remote and exotic music.

"I could have sworn it was a gypsy violin," Chester told me. "I thought perhaps a caravan was passing by, so I ran to the window."

I remembered my mother telling me something about caravans when I was a puppy. But for the life of me, I couldn't remember what.

"What's a caravan?" I asked, feeling a little stupid.

"A caravan is a band of gypsies traveling through the forest in their wagons," Chester answered.

"Ah, yes." It was coming back to me now. "Station wagons?"

"No, covered wagons! The gypsies travel all through the land, setting up camps around great bonfires, doing magical tricks, and sometimes, if you cross their palms with a piece of silver, they'll tell your fortune."

"You mean if I gave them a fork, they'd tell my fortune?" I asked, breathlessly.

Chester looked at me with disdain. "Save your silverware," he said. "It wasn't a caravan after all."

I was disappointed. "What was it?" I asked.

Chester explained that when he looked out the window, he saw Professor Mickelwhite, our next door neighbor, playing the violin in his living room. He listened for a few moments to the haunting melody and sighed with relief. I've really got to stop reading these horror stories late at night, he thought. It's beginning to affect my mind. He yawned and turned to go back to his chair and get some sleep. As he turned, however, he was startled by what he saw.

There in the moonlight, as the music filtered through the air, sat the bunny, his eyes intense and staring, an unearthly aura about them.

"Now, this is the part you won't believe," Chester said to me, "but as I watched, his lips parted in a hideous smile, and where a rabbit's buck teeth should have been, two little pointed fangs glistened."

I wasn't sure what to make of Chester's story, but the way he told it, it set my hair on end.

Three
SOME UNUSUAL
GOINGS-ON

The next few days passed uneventfully. I was very bored. Our new arrival slept all day, and Chester, whose curiosity had been aroused by the strange behavior of the rabbit that first night, had decided to stay awake every night to observe him. Therefore, he, too, spent most of his days sleeping. So *I* had no one to talk to.

The evenings weren't much better. Toby and Pete, who used to play with me as soon as they got home from school, now ran immediately to that silly rabbit's cage to play with him. Or at least they'd try to.

Bunnicula did not make the most energetic playmate. It took him quite a while to wake up each night and then when he did awaken, he didn't do much except hop around the living room. He didn't play catch, he didn't fetch, he didn't roll over to get his tummy rubbed. I couldn't understand why they played with him at all. I expect it was because he was new and different. But I was confident that they would soon tire of him and come back to trusty ol' Harold.

Finally, on the morning of the fourth day, I caught Chester bleary-eyed over the water dish. He grumbled at me in a most unpleasant manner.

"You know, Chester, you were never exactly charming in the morning, but lately you've become downright grumpy."

Chester growled in response.

"What are you doing this for anyway? What are you looking for? He's just a cute little bunny."

"Cute little bunny!" Chester was amazed at my character analysis. "That's what you think. He's a danger to this household and everyone in it."

"Oh, Chester," I said, with an indulgent smile, "I think your reading has gone to your head."

"It's just because I do read that I know what I'm talking about."

"Well, what are you talking about? I still don't understand."

"I'm not sure yet, but I know there's something funny about that rabbit. That's why I have to keep alert."

"But look at you—you're exhausted. You sleep all the time. How can you call that alert?"

"I'm awake when it's important. He sleeps all day, so I sleep all day."

"So just what have you seen since that first night that makes you uneasy?"

"Well . . . " said Chester, "I, uh . . . that is . . ." At this point, Chester started to bathe his tail, which is a cat's way of changing a subject he finds uncomfortable. He then stumbled sleepily into the living room.

"So?" I asked again, following him, "what have you seen?"

"Nothing!" he snapped, and proceeded to curl up on his chair to go to sleep. After a moment, he opened one eye. "But that doesn't mean there's nothing *to* see."

For the next few mornings, it was the same

routine. I'd be ready for a good romp around the living room, and Chester would go to sleep. Pete and Toby were at school. Mr. Monroe was at the university (he never did too much romping around, anyway). And Mrs. Monroe was at her office.

No one to play with poor, neglected Harold. At first, I thought I could strike up a friendship with Bunnicula and maybe teach him a few tricks. But I could never wake him up. He was always waking up just about sunset, when I wanted to take a snooze. A rabbit, I concluded, is cute to look at, but is generally useless, especially as a companion to dogs. So, I would retire each day with my favorite shoe to the rug and chew.

Now, some people (especially Mr. and Mrs. Monroe) can't understand my taste for shoes and yell at me for snacking on them. But I always say there's no accounting for taste. For instance, I remember one evening when Mr. Monroe picked some of his sour balls out of the bowl by his chair and dropped a green one on the floor. He didn't notice as it rolled across the room and landed near my nose. I decided this was a perfect opportunity to try one for myself. I placed it in my mouth . . . and wished immediately that I hadn't. As the tears started running out of my eyes, I thought, What's wrong with my mouth?! It's turning inside out!

Mr. Monroe immediately noticed that something had happened. "What's the matter, Harold? Are you looking for someone to kiss?"

"Help! Help!" I wanted to cry, but all that came out was an "*ooooo*" sound. I "*ooooo*"-ed for days.

So how can anyone who likes green sourballs criticize me for preferring a nice penny loafer or a bedroom slipper?

But back to the matter at hand:

One morning, Chester had news.

"That bunny," he whispered to me across our food bowls, "got out of his cage last night."

"Don't be ridiculous," I said. "How could he break through that wire? Look how little he is."

"That's just it! He didn't break through any wire. He got out of his cage without breaking anything, or opening any doors!"

I looked puzzled. So Chester told me the following story.

"Now, Harold," he said, "I don't want you thinking I'm not a good watchcat, but after a few hours last night, I grew curious about the time. I went into the hallway and . . . you know that new clock they've got? The big one? That goes all the way to the ceiling? Well, see, it has this thing in the middle called a pendulum. At first, I figured I would just leave it alone. It looked like that spool they tied on a string and hung from the doorknob for me to play with when I was a kitten. Everytime I hit that silly spool with my paw, it would swing back and hit me on the nose. I hated that toy. So naturally, when I saw this one, I decided not to have anything to do with it. I checked the time. It was midnight. I was all set to go back to the living room when something stopped me."

"Curiosity?" I ventured.

"I suppose you could call it that. I prefer to think of it as the challenge of the unknown. I put one paw over my nose and reached out with the other one and gave it one good smack. I darn near broke my arm. It's still tender; see how swollen it is."

He showed me his little paw. I couldn't see anything wrong. But I knew better than to argue with him. "Oh yes," I said, "that looks terrible. You must be suffering awfully. You'd better go easy today."

He limped dramatically, just far enough to display his new handicap, and continued.

"I couldn't even get to the pendulum. Somebody had put glass in front of it, and I was pretty mad. I was all set to go back, but at the same time, I couldn't help watching the thing move back and forth, back and forth. Back and forth . . . It was so easy to watch, and before I knew what had happened, I was waking up."

"You fell asleep?" I asked incredulously.

"I couldn't help it. I didn't even know it had happened. But I looked up at the face of the clock and it was twelve forty-five! I'd been gone forty-five minutes. I ran back into the living room, looked at Bunnicula's cage, and it was empty. I couldn't imagine where he was. Then I noticed a light coming from under the kitchen door. I went into a crouch, stalking the light, when . . . *click* . . . I heard the refrigerator door close, and the light went out."

"It must have been Mr. Monroe having his midnight snack," I suggested.

"No, that's what I thought. I jumped on my chair, curled up real quick and kept one eye open, pretending to be asleep. Slowly, the door to the kitchen squeaked open. This little head poked out from around the corner and looked to either side to see if the coast was clear. Then . . . guess who came bouncing out all by himself, and with that idiotic grin of his plastered all over his face?"

"Well . . . I guess it wasn't Mr. Monroe," I said.

"Not unless he wears bunny pajamas and gets very tiny at night."

"Bunnicula, huh?"

"You got it. Unfortunately, I hadn't positioned myself so that I could see him get back into the cage. And I didn't want to let him know that I had seen anything, so I had to stay put. I still don't know how he got out, or back in."

At this point, Mr. Monroe came downstairs to make breakfast.

I wondered if Chester hadn't dreamed the whole thing. He did admit he'd fallen asleep and, as I've said, he has quite an imagination. But I was game. After all, there hadn't been any excitement in this place for days. Chester and I took our positions under the kitchen table. We didn't have long to wait.

"Holy cow!" Mr. Monroe yelped as he opened the refrigerator door. He took this funny-looking

white thing out of the fridge and held it at arm's
length.

"Peter, come down here!"

"What is that?" I whispered.

"Beats me," Chester answered. "It looks like a white tomato."

"Very funny," I said, as Pete came into the kitchen.

"Peter, have you been playing with your chemistry set in here?"

"No, Dad, why?"

"I thought this might be one of your experiments. Do you know what it is?"

"Gee, Dad, it looks like a white tomato."

Just then, Mrs. Monroe and Toby came in the door.

"What's all the fuss about?" Mrs. Monroe asked.

"We were just trying to figure out what this is."

Toby pulled it down so he could get a better look.

"Well," he said, "it looks to me like a white tomato."

Mr. Monroe took a good long look. "You know," he said to his wife, "it really does look like a white tomato."

"There's one way to find out," said Mrs. Monroe, who always was the practical one. "Let's cut it open and see what's inside."

Everybody gathered around the table. I jumped up on a chair, and in all the excitement, no one noticed that I had my paws on the table (which under normal circumstances was discouraged, to say the least). Chester wasn't so lucky.

"Chester, get off the table," Mrs. Monroe said. Chester jumped onto Toby's shoulders, where he stayed to view the proceedings.

Mrs. Monroe took her sharpest knife and cut cleanly through the thing. It fell into two halves.

"It's a tomato, all right," said Mrs. Monroe. "Here are the seeds."

"But it's all white," Toby observed.

"And look," said Pete, "it's dry."

"So it is," Mr. Monroe said, as he picked up one of the halves. "There is no juice at all. Well, Ann, what do you think?"

"It's gone bad, I guess, though I've never heard of a tomato turning white before. Come on," she said, clearing the table, "let's throw it out and have breakfast. And Harold, get your paws off the table."

Rats.

Chester jumped down from Toby's shoulders and motioned for me to follow him into the living room.

"This had better be important," I said. "They're cooking bacon."

"A white tomato. Very significant," Chester murmured.

"So it's a white tomato," I said, edging my way back to the kitchen door. "What does that have to do with Bunnicula?"

"I can tell you one thing," Chester said. "I got a good look at the tomato. There were very suspicious marks on the skin."

"So?"

"I believe they're teeth marks."

"So?"

"So tonight I'm going to reread a book I read last year."

"How fascinating," I said, as the aroma of frying bacon wafted across my nostrils. "And what book might that be?"

"The Mark of the Vampire!"

"What!" I stopped dead in my tracks.

"Meet me tonight after the others have gone to sleep. You'd better take a nap today so you can stay awake."

Chester closed his eyes. I shifted my look to Bunnicula, who seemed to be asleep in this cage. A tiny smile sat upon his lips. A happy dream? I wondered. Or something else?

My reverie was broken by the sound of crunching bacon. I was in the kitchen in a flash.

A CAT PREPARES

I almost didn't make it to my meeting with Chester that night. Toby had a feast in his room. It was Friday night, and on Friday nights, Toby gets to stay up and read as late as he wants to. So, of course, he needs lots of food to keep up his strength. Good food like cheese crackers, chocolate cupcakes (my very favorite, the kind with cream in the middle, *mmmm*!), pretzels, and peanut butter sandwiches. The last I cannot abide because my mouth always gets stuck. Chocolate cupcakes with cream in the center, however, are another story.

This particular evening, I stationed myself on

Toby's stomach. Usually, I'm a little more subtle but, having missed out on the bacon at breakfast, I was not about to take any chances on the chocolate cupcakes (with cream in the center).

Toby knew what I was after. But sometimes he thinks he's funny, and he plays little games with me.

"Hi, Harold, I'll bet you'd like a peanut butter sandwich, wouldn't you? Here, you have this one that's leftover from yesterday, while I eat this boring old chocolate cupcake—which is nice and fresh and has cream in the middle. Okay, Harold?"

Ha ha. My sides are splitting.

"What's the matter? Don't you want the peanut butter sandwich? All right, I'll put it away for another night. Oh, here's something you might like. It's a green sourball from Dad's candy dish that was stuck to my sock. Would you like that, huh, pal?"

Oh boy, the kid is really hot tonight.

"No, huh? Well, I'd give you one of my cupcakes, but I know how much you hate chocolate."

Would a little drooling on your stomach help convince you otherwise?

"Oh, you like chocolate! Okay then, you can have both of them!"

37

A CAT PREPARES

One thing I have to say about Toby: Although he's got a rotten sense of humor, he's a nice kid. Naturally, once I'd eaten both cupcakes (which took approximately four seconds), I felt obliged to hang around and let Toby know I was grateful. What better way than to share a few of his cheese crackers?

"Well, Harold," Toby said some time later, "we've had quite a party, but I have to go to sleep now. I can't keep my eyes open, so I'll have to wait until tomorrow to find out what happens in the next chapter. This is a good book, Harold. It's called *Treasure Island*, and it's by a man named Robert Louis Stevenson. It's kind of hard reading, though. I have to keep looking the big words up in the dictionary, so it's taking me a long time to get through it."

I've always had trouble with words myself. Half the time they don't mean what I think they're going to, and then, even when I do find out what they mean, I forget the next day anyway. You might say that I'm smart—but just not the scholarly type.

"But it's a really good story," Toby continued. "It's all about pirates and this little boy just like me."

No dogs?

"And a parrot, Harold."

A parrot? What's a parrot? Is there anything about chocolate cake? That's my idea of a treasure.

"Well, good night, Harold. If you're going to sleep here, you'll have to get off my stomach because it's a little full right now."

Good night, Toby.

I curled up at the foot of the bed, but I couldn't sleep trying to figure out what a parrot was. I thought it might be a lady pirate, since the words sounded something alike, but then again, I thought it might be an umbrella. Chester would know, I thought, so I went downstairs to ask him.

"Well, you certainly took your time," Chester snapped as I sauntered casually into the room. "I finished my book half an hour ago. Where were you?"

"It so happens I was discussing great works of literature with Toby."

"Since when is a Twinkies wrapper considered a great work of literature?"

I decided to ignore that. Unfortunately, several chocolate crumbs fell from my mouth to the floor at precisely that moment.

"As a matter of fact," I said, trying valiantly to

regain my dignity, "we were talking about *Treasure Island*. Ever hear of it?"

"Ever hear of it?" he sneered. "I read *that* when I was a kitten."

"Oh. Then, tell me, Chester, what is a parrot?"

Chester looked at me scornfully. "A parrot," he said, "is a tropical zygodactyl bird (order psittaciformes) that has a stout curved hooked bill, is often crested, brightly variegated, and an excellent mimic. In other words, Harold, a parrot is a little bird with a big mouth."

"Oh," I said after a moment. "I thought maybe it was an umbrella."

"Did you get so busy discussing parrots with Toby that you forgot you were going to meet me here? This is important, Harold."

I still wasn't sure what a parrot was, but I decided this was not the time to pursue it.

"Come over here," Chester commanded, indicating his chair, "and let me show you this book."

I looked at the chair. Chester was already sitting in it, with a very large book open in front of him.

"I don't think there's going to be room for both of us, Chester," I said.

"Come on, come on, you're wasting time. Just jump up here."

I surveyed the scene carefully. I knew I would have to get a running start since there was just a tiny spot left for me and I would never be able to fit into it if I pulled myself up slowly. Apparently, I was taking too long for Chester's liking.

"Will you get up here?" he hissed.

Okay, if that's what you want. I ran and jumped onto the chair, landing with a great kerplop.

"Chester, where are you?" I cried. I couldn't see anything but the back of the chair. I'd forgotten to turn myself around.

"I'm here, you great oaf!"

I turned my head. "What are you doing on the floor?" I asked.

"You knocked me off the chair. Now just stay put. I'm coming back up."

I moved to the back of the chair, and Chester landed on the front.

"Now, let's see," he said, "we both have to see the book. You come over here, and I'll move this way."

I don't know if you've ever watched a cat try to decide where to sit, but it involves a lot of circling around, sitting, getting up again, circling some more, thinking about it, lying down, standing up, bathing a paw or tail and . . . circling! A dog, on the other hand, sits. "This looks like a good spot," a dog will say to himself. He will then lower his body to the spot in question and is usually so secure in his decision that he will fall asleep immediately.

Chester took what felt like twenty minutes to settle himself in, and just as I was drifting off, the kicks started. "Come on, Harold, quit hogging the seat. And wake up. What were you trying to do? Take a little cat nap? Ha ha ha."

I yawned.

"Now," said Chester, turning to the book, "let's get down to brass tacks."

"What exactly is on your mind?" I asked.

"This book and that rabbit," Chester replied. "Now tell me, Harold, have you noticed anything funny about that rabbit?"

"No," I said, "but I've certainly noticed a lot of funny things about you recently."

"Think about it. That rabbit sleeps all day."

"So do I. So do you."

"Furthermore, he's got funny little sharp teeth."

"So do I. So do you."

"Furthermore, he gets in and out of his cage by himself. What kind of rabbit can do that?"

"A smart one," I said. "I could do it."

"We're not talking about you, Harold. We're talking about the rabbit. Now, where did they find him?"

"At the movies."

"Yes, but *what* movie?"

"*Dracula,*" I said, "so?"

"So," he said quickly, "remember the note around his neck? What language was it in?"

"An obscure dialect of the Carpathian mountain region," I answered smugly. He didn't know everything.

"Ah ha!" Chester said, "but what *area* of the Carpathian mountain region?"

Area? What's an area? I looked at him blankly.

"Transylvania!" he cried triumphantly. "And that proves my point."

"What point? What are we talking about?"

"And don't forget the white tomato! That's most important of all!"

"But, what . . ."

"This book," said Chester, disregarding me, "tells us just what we need to know."

"*What?*" I practically screamed. "What does it tell us? What does this book have to do with Bunnicula? What are you talking about? What's going on here? I can't stand it anymore!"

Chester regarded me coolly. "You're really very

excitable, Harold. That's not good for your blood pressure."

I put my paws around his throat. "Tell me," I said in a low, threatening voice, "or I'll squeeze you till you pop."

"Okay, okay, don't get upset. Now this book tells you everything you've always wanted to know about vampires but were afraid to ask."

Personally, I had never wanted to know anything about vampires, but at the moment, I was afraid to tell that to Chester.

"I still don't understand what vampires have to do with our little furry friend."

"One," Chester said, "vampires do not sleep at night. They sleep only during the day. The same holds true for this rabbit. Two, vampires can get in and out of locked rooms. Bunnicula gets in and out of his locked cage."

This was beginning to interest me. "Didn't you say something about the refrigerator?"

"That's right. He got the refrigerator open . . . all by himself. Three, vampires have long pointed teeth. They're called fangs."

"Well, don't we have fangs?"

"No, we have canines. That's different."

"What's different about it?"

"Fangs are more pointed, and vampires use fangs to bite people on the neck."

"Yech! Who'd want to do that?"

"Vampires would, that's who."

"Wait a minute. I saw Mrs. Monroe bite Mr. Monroe on the neck once. Does that mean she's a vampire?"

"Boy, are you dumb. She's not a vampire. She's a lawyer."

"She bites necks."

"I don't think that's quite the same thing. Now, Bunnicula does not bite people on the neck. At least, not so far. But he does bite vegetables . . ."

"On the neck?" I asked.

"Vegetables don't have necks, Harold. Vegetables are like that. It's like dogs. Dogs don't have brains. Dogs are like that."

"Oh yeah?" I said. "Of course he bites vegetables. All rabbits bite vegetables."

"He *bites* them, Harold, but he does not eat them. That tomato was all white. What does that mean?"

"It means . . . that he paints vegetables?" I ventured.

"It means he bites vegetables to make a hole in them, and then he sucks out all the juices."

"But what about all the lettuce and carrots that Toby has been feeding him in his cage?"

"Ah ha, what indeed!" Chester said. "Look at this!" Whereupon, he stuck his paw under the chair cushion and brought out with a flourish an assortment of strange white objects. Some of them looked like unironed handkerchiefs, and the others . . . well, the others didn't look like anything I'd ever seen before.

"What are they?" I asked.

Chester smiled. "Lettuce and carrots," he said. "*White* lettuce and carrots. I found them hidden behind his cage."

I was aghast. What did it all mean? Could Chester be right? Was this harmless looking little ball of fluff really a vampire? Just then, Chester let out a yelp.

"Look," he said, "the cage is empty again. Oh, we're fools, we're fools! We've let him get out of our sight. It's your fault."

"My fault! You're the one who took twenty minutes to sit down."

"Well, if you hadn't knocked me off in the first place—"

"Wait a minute, why are we arguing? Let's find Bunnicula."

Just then, we heard a click in the kitchen.

"Refrigerator," I whispered. Chester nodded. We jumped down and moved cautiously to the kitchen door.

"Sshhh," Chester warned unnecessarily as we crept along, "don't make any noise. We don't want him to hear us coming."

"Obviously," I retorted.

The light went out under the door.

"He must have closed the refrigerator," Chester said. "Easy now." We pushed the door open. The kitchen was dark. There was not a sound.

"Pssst, Chester . . ."

"What?"

"I can't see."

"I can. But I can't see *him.*"

"He's not here."

There was a soft scamper across the linoleum, and we turned just in time to see a little white tail bounce out the door into the living room.

"Drat! We've missed him. Come on, Harold, let's see if we can catch up with him." Chester started toward the door.

"Wait, Chester, what's that on the floor by the refrigerator?"

He turned. This new object interested him more than following Bunnicula. "Watch out," he said, "I'll take care of this." He slunk across the room slowly, muscles taut, eyes alert. When he was about six inches away, he stuck out his paw, closed his eyes, and batted at the object tentatively. I don't think he made any contact.

"Get closer," I said.

Chester's eyes popped open. "Who's the cat here?" he asked. "I know what I'm doing." And he proceeded to bat the air three more times.

"What is it?" I squealed, as my throat contracted in fear.

"I don't know yet, but whatever it is, it's not alive."

"Oh boy, if I wait for you, we'll be here all night." I walked bravely to the object and sniffed it.

"Well?" asked Chester.

"Beats me."

Chester came closer. After a moment of close examination, he gasped.

I jumped. I could feel my heart pounding in my chest.

"Harold . . . " Chester blurted.

"What? What?"

"It's . . ."

"Yes?"

"It's . . ."

"What is it, Chester?!"

"It's a white zucchini!"

CHESTER GOES
INTO HIS ACT

The next morning, I was awakened by a scream. "Robert! Robert, come down here right away. There's something wrong in the kitchen!"

For a moment, panic seized me. I thought she'd run out of dog food. But then I remembered the events of the previous evening.

Mr. Monroe came bounding down the stairs. "Chester! Chester!" I cried. "Did you see Mr. Monroe? His face has turned white! It's Bunnicula, isn't it?"

"No," he said calmly, "it's shaving cream, you idiot."

By now, the excitement in the kitchen was at full

throttle. The table was covered with Bunnicula's handiwork. There were white beans and white peas and white squash and white tomatoes and white lettuce and white zucchini.

"What can it mean, Robert?" Mrs. Monroe was saying. "I'm getting worried. One tomato is a curiosity, but this is unheard of."

"There must be something wrong with our refrigerator. That's it. It's turning all the vegetables white."

"But look," she said, "I left these tomatoes on the windowsill, and they're white, too. And this squash I left in the bowl on the table."

At that moment, Pete and Toby came into the kitchen.

"Holy cow! What's going on?"

"Hey! Maybe it's a vegetable blight, Mom."

"Could that be, Robert? Did you ever hear of anything like that?"

"Well . . . uh . . . no, actually . . . that is, I've heard of blight, but nothing like this."

Chester leaned my way. "This will take forever if we leave it up to them. Sometimes, human beings can be so slow." I started to answer him, but he was heading for the table.

"What about that friend of yours in the Agriculture Department?"

"Oh, Tom Cragin?"

"Could we call him and ask him if we're doing something wrong?"

"It's DDT, Mom," Peter interjected. "I know about this stuff. It's because you buy vegetables that aren't organic."

"All vegetables are organic, Peter," Mrs. Monroe replied.

"That's not what my teacher says. See, Toby, I told you this would happen. They're using chemicals on our food, and if you're not careful, you'll turn white, too."

"Like Dad?"

"Robert, couldn't you take that shaving cream off your face?"

"Oh yes, of course. Where's my towel? I know I brought it down with me."

For that matter, where was Chester? I'd seen him going toward the table, but I'd lost track of him listening to all that talk about DDT. I just hoped they didn't use any of that stuff where they grew chocolate cupcakes.

"Pete, did you take my towel?"

"Why would I take your towel, Dad? I don't shave."

Just then, the door swung open. I could not believe my eyes. There was Chester, with Mr. Monroe's towel draped across his back and tied under his neck like a cape. That was strange enough, but on his face was an expression that sent chills down my spine. His eyes were wide and staring. The corners of his mouth were pulled back in an evil grimace. His teeth were bared and gleaming in the morning light. He cackled menacingly and threw back his head as if he were laughing at all of us. I thought he'd completely lost his mind.

"There's my towel. What's the matter, Chester, were you cold?" Mr. Monroe bent down to take the towel from Chester. Before he could lay his hands on it, Chester flipped over onto his back, closed his eyes and folded his paws over his chest. It was a hideous sight. He opened his eyes wide. With paws outstretched, he . . . slowly . . . lifted . . . his . . . head . . . his eyes glazed and vacant. Soon the upper half of his body followed, all in one smooth flow, until he was in a sitting position.

"Hey, Dad, did you leave your brandy glass out last night? Chester is acting a little weird."

"Well, son, cats are funny creatures . . ."

I glanced at Chester. He wasn't laughing.

"Psst, Chester. What are you up to?"

"I'm a vampire, you dolt. Can't you tell? I'm trying to warn them."

"Well, it's not working. You'd better think of something else." Chester frowned, apparently deep in thought.

". . . so you see, Toby," Mr. Monroe was explaining, "all cats are as individual as all people. Maybe he just wants to get our attention. Isn't that right, kitty-cat?" Ordinarily, Chester would have left the room upon being called "kitty-cat," but he was lost in thought.

"Come on, Chester, give me back my towel." Mr. Monroe moved toward Chester. Chester's eyes lit up. He looked at me and smiled. I sensed I was not going to like what he had in mind. I was toying with the notion of slinking under the table when Chester fixed me with his eyes. How deep they were, like black pools. I felt myself floating, lost in them, my will no longer my own. I felt an inexplicable urge to murmur "Yes, Master," when he walked slowly, steadily toward me. As he drew nearer, I found myself unable to move. He stopped before me, never taking his gaze from me, and lunged.

"YEOW!!!"

"Mom, Chester bit Harold on the neck!"

"Aw, that wasn't a real bite, was it, Chester? That was a love bite. Isn't that cute?"

Love bite, my foot. That hurt!

"Chester, what's the matter with you?" I sputtered. "Do I look like a tomato?"

"Oh, it doesn't matter anyway, Harold. They don't understand. How can human beings read the same books I do and still be so thick?"

Our conversation was interrupted. Mrs. Monroe picked Chester up and cuddled him. I was praying she would not add insult to injury by kissing his nose, which he hates more than anything.

"Poor Chester, do you need a little love? Do you know what I'm going to do, you big ball of fuzz, you?" Oh, oh. I could tell what was coming. "I'm going to kiss you on your little nose." Yep, I could tell that was coming, all right. Chester knew better than to resist. He went limp in Mrs. Monroe's arms. Mr. Monroe took his towel off Chester.

"I still don't know why he's wearing my towel," he said.

"I think he must be cold, dear. Here's your towel. Why don't you get his kitty sweater . . ." Chester looked ill. ". . . and he can wear that all day."

As Chester was being buttoned into his bright yellow sweater (with little purple mice in cowboy hats all over it), Mr. Monroe said, "What about those vegetables? Shall I speak to Tom Cragin?"

"Yes, dear," Mrs. Monroe said, "why don't you? I'm sure there's some explanation. In the meantime, I'll change markets. To tell you the truth, I'm really much more worried about Chester. We'd better keep our eye on him."

Chester and I did not speak until late afternoon. I was busy nursing my neck, and Chester was busy hiding under the sofa, too embarrassed to be seen. When we did speak at last, it was a brief exchange.

"Hey, Chester," I called when he finally crawled out from under, "we don't have to worry about any vampire bunnies anymore. All you have to do is stand outside his cage in that sweater, and he'll laugh himself to death."

Chester was not amused. "That's right, make fun.

All of you. No one understands. I tried to warn them, and they wouldn't heed. Now, I'm going to take matters into my own hands."

Whereupon, Chester and his sixteen purple mice went into the kitchen for dinner.

Six

HAROLD
HELPS OUT

That night, I had an uneasy sleep. Strange noises emanated from downstairs. It sounded like toenails were clicking back and forth on the floor. It must be Bunnicula making his midnight run, I thought, although I'd never known him to make a sound. And I smelled the funniest odor in the air—something familiar, though I couldn't place it. As the night progressed, it grew stronger and stronger until finally it tickled my nose and I sneezed myself awake. I jumped off Toby's bed, still sniffling, and headed down the stairs for the living room to find Chester, to see if he could smell it, too.

The odor grew even stronger as I approached the living room. Standing in the doorway was Chester, a strange pendant hanging from his neck.

"Phew, Chester," I said, "what are you wearing that awful thing for? It smells!"

"Of course it smells," he replied. "Here, I made one for you, too. Put it on."

"Are you kidding? That thing smells like garlic."

"It is garlic," Chester stated matter-of-factly.

"Why are you wearing garlic?" I asked, thinking that by this time Chester was capable of anything. As we walked into the living room, I tripped on another piece of garlic lying in the doorway.

"Careful," said Chester, "watch your step."

I surveyed the room and saw that it was strewn with garlic. On the doorways . . . over the windows . . . and around Bunnicula's cage. The poor little fellow had buried his nose as far as possible under his blanket.

I was about to follow his example and return to Toby's bed to bury my nose under the blankets when Chester grabbed my tail with his teeth.

"You're not leaving this room until you put this on," he grumbled at me. I think that's what he said. I wasn't sure because he had my tail in his mouth.

"It's not polite to talk with your mouth full, Chester. Drop that tail." Meanwhile, my eyes were beginning to water.

"Listen," Chester snapped at me (fortunately letting go of my tail first), "the book said to use garlic."

"What book?" I asked. *The Joy of Cooking?*

Chester continued, *"The Mark of the Vampire* says garlic renders vampires immobile."

"What does that mean?"

"It means they can't go anywhere if there's garlic around."

"Well, I've got news for you, Chester. I can't go anywhere either. The smell is killing me—"

"But you've got to put it on; it says so in the book. If you don't put it on, I'll put it on for you."

"Doe, Chester," I said as my nose suddenly and involuntarily closed, "I'be leaving dis roob right dow." And I did.

I was so sick to my stomach from the aroma that I decided to spend the early morning hours outdoors. As dawn approached, it seemed that it would be a peaceful day. The sky was clear, the birds were singing, and I felt contented after my difficult night just to be lying in the grass, feeling the ladybugs crawl up my ears. Suddenly, the calm was broken. Strange piercing screams came from the area of the kitchen. Not again, I thought. What's turned white now?

As it happened, it was Chester. There in the sink, lathered with soap, was the feline detective, yelling his head off. Mrs. Monroe was scrubbing him vigorously and, from the sound of her voice, was in the middle of a long lecture.

"I don't know what's gotten into you, Chester. You never played with garlic before. I thought you hated the smell of it, and here you've gotten it all over yourself. Stop wriggling, you'll get soap in your eyes. If you want to chew on something, I'll get you some catnip. But stay out of my herbs!" Then she rinsed him off, rubbed him with a towel, and plunked him down in front of the stove to finish drying.

"Shut the door," he hissed at me. "I'm freezing. That silly woman, doesn't she know *cats don't get baths*?"

"What do you mean? I get baths all the time," I said, closing the door with my back foot.

"That's because you're too dumb to bathe yourself. Cats always bathe themselves, it's a rule. Everyone knows that."

"Well, at least it smells nice in here again." I sniffed as I settled down next to Chester by the stove. "And it's all toasty warm here in the kitchen."

"Sure it smells nice again," he said, "but now the house isn't safe anymore."

"What do you mean?" I asked, getting closer.

"I mean, it worked last night. The garlic worked. No more vegetables turned white, did they?"

"No, but . . ."

"That means Bunnicula didn't get out of his cage last night."

"Maybe he was just tired," I said, "or maybe he was full."

"Don't be ridiculous," he replied. "It was the garlic. He *couldn't* leave his cage. But tonight he'll be free to roam again, and I've got to find a way to stop him that isn't smelly."

Mr. and Mrs. Monroe were hurrying in and out of the room, stepping over us, late for work. Mrs. Monroe yelled up to Toby, "Don't forget to take the steak out of the freezer when you get home today, Toby, and leave it on the table to defrost. And this time, remember to put a plate under it."

Chester's ears perked up. "Of course!" he said. "That's what I'll do." And he strolled past me with a knowing smile. Mrs. Monroe turned off the stove and left the room. It was too much for me to figure out, so I went to sleep on the nice, warm kitchen floor.

I was awakened by a bite on the ear. Chester was sitting by me, looking very impatient.

"Boy, nothing wakes you up," he said. "I've been yelling and poking at you for ten minutes."

"I was dreaming," I answered defensively, "about a place where there weren't any cats around to bother nice dogs and wake them up when they needed their rest."

"You can finish sleeping later," he said crisply. "Right now, you have to help me."

"Do what?" I asked.

"Get Bunnicula out of the cage."

I sprang back. "Get him out of the cage?! I thought that was what you didn't want. I thought you said he was dangerous. What if he attacks me?"

"Aren't you ashamed?" Chester replied. "Afraid of a harmless little bunny?"

"Harmless? I thought you said he was a threat to this house and everyone in it. Isn't that what you said? Isn't that what we've been talking about all this time?"

"He is a threat, but only at night. During the day he's just a very sleepy rabbit, and that's why we have to do it now, while the sun is still up. Follow me," he said. "There isn't much time. Toby stayed down here forever, and the others will be home soon. Boy, you must have been tired, Harold. You slept through lunch."

I followed Chester into the living room. My heart was pounding as he unlocked the cage door with his paw. (It looked as if he'd had years of experience opening locks.)

The door swung open; Bunnicula was sleeping peacefully. He did, however, look a little green around the gills, probably from the garlic. I was just wondering how a rabbit could have gills when Chester said, "Okay, Harold, do your stuff while I get what I need from the kitchen."

"Well, what do you want me to do? I can't read your mind."

"Get him out of the cage and onto the floor, and I'll be right back," Chester said.

What? What?

"What?" I verbalized. "How am I supposed to do that?"

"Use your head," he answered. And he was gone.

Looking at the cage, I realized that was precisely what I would have to do.

Until this moment, I had never had to face the possibility of actual physical contact with a real, live rabbit. I looked upon my chore reluctantly. I seemed to recall my grandfather telling me that one picked a rabbit up by its neck with one's teeth. This I attempted, though the very idea set my stomach churning. I squeezed my head through the tiny door and gently placed my teeth around the skin of the bunny's neck. To avoid any suggestion of violence (I've never been one for the sport of hunting), I preferred to think of myself as the creature's mother, carrying it off to safety. Unfortunately, I couldn't carry it anywhere, for once my head was in the cage, it wouldn't come out again. I could go neither forward nor backward.

At that moment, Chester appeared at the door, carrying in his mouth what looked every bit like a nice, big, juicy raw steak. My eyes popped, my teeth dropped Bunnicula, my mouth opened, and I began to drool. After all, I *had* missed lunch.

"Chester, what are you doing with that steak?"

"Haven't you gotten him out of there yet?"

"I can't get either of us out of here. My head's
stuck."

"Oh, Harold, sometimes I despair. Here, I'll get
you both out. I should have done everything
myself."

He came over, dropped the steak just a few feet
away from me, and climbed up on my shoulders. "You
pull your head out while I push against the cage."

"Who gets the steak?" I asked.

"Don't worry about the steak, Harold. Just pull."

"I would have more motivation if I knew who is
to get the steak."

Chester ignored me. I pulled. He pushed. I felt
something go POP! We all fell in a jumble: Chester,
the cage, Bunnicula, and me. When I looked around,
Bunnicula was lying next to me, still sound asleep.

"There you are," I said. "We got him out. Now,
let's eat."

"No dice," Chester said. "Just read this to me so
I'll be sure I'm doing it right." And he handed me a
book. *That* book, *again.*

"Start at the top of the page," Chester said as he
picked up the steak.

"Why don't *you* read, and I'll hold the steak?"

"Mmphph," Chester replied. I took it to mean that I was to start reading.

"'To destroy the vampire and end his reign of terror, it is necessary to pound a sharp stake . . .'"

Chester interrupted. "A sharp steak?" he asked. "What does that mean?"

"I'll taste it and tell you if it's sharp," I offered.

"Oh, never mind. This will do. It's sirloin. Keep reading."

"'. . . to pound a sharp stake into the vampire's heart. This must be done during the daylight hours, when the vampire has no powers.'"

"Okay," he said, "this is it. I'm sorry I had to go this far, but if they'd listened, this wouldn't have been necessary." He dragged the steak across the floor and laid it across the inert bunny. Then with his paws, he began to hit the steak.

"Are you sure this is what they mean, Chester?"

"Am I anywhere near his heart?" he asked.

"It's hard to tell," I said. "All I can really see are his nose and his ears. You know, he's really sort of cute."

Chester was getting that glint in his eyes again. He was pounding away at the steak, harder and harder.

"Be careful," I cried, "you'll hurt him."

Chester increased his attack. I was really getting worried when the door opened and Mr. and Mrs. Monroe were suddenly with us in the room.

"Chester!" Mrs. Monroe screamed. "What are you doing with my dinner? Robert, get that steak away from Chester. And what's the matter with Bunnicula? Why is he on the floor?"

Mr. Monroe took the beautiful steak away. I wished it a fond farewell with tears in my eyes. As the kitchen door swung open, Chester whispered with cold determination, "All right, the last resort!" and dashed into the kitchen. Seconds later, he was back, carrying his water dish between his teeth. He ran toward Bunnicula and with a mad yowl threw the dish of water at the rabbit. Unfortunately, he was so hysterical that his aim was not the best. With water dripping from my ears, I watched Mrs. Monroe pick Chester up by the scruff of his neck and toss him unceremoniously out the front door.

"Robert, we are going to have to do something about that cat. Look at this mess. Dinner's ruined, the poor bunny is out of his cage, and Harold is sopping wet." I tried to look as pathetic as I knew how.

"Aw, poor Harold," Mrs. Monroe cooed as she

dried me off. "You've had a rough day . . . you and
Bunnicula. I don't know what's the matter with
your friend. But unless he learns how to behave,
he'll just have to spend the night outside."

Mr. Monroe meanwhile had restored Bunnicula
to his cage and the cage to the windowsill. I couldn't
believe it when I saw that Bunnicula was still asleep.

"Ann," Mr. Monroe said, "the steak is ruined.
Why don't we let Harold have it? He deserves a
treat anyway, don't you, ol' boy?"

I panted appropriately.

After my delicious dinner, I turned my attention to
the book still lying open on the floor.

"'Another method of destroying the vampire is
to immerse the body in water. The body will then
shrivel and disappear, as the vampire emits one last
scream of terror.'"

Whew, I thought, so that's what he was trying to
do. Thank goodness he missed. I had no regrets
about missing a scene like that. Poor Bunnicula.

I looked over toward the cage, and there on the
other side of the window was a pathetic tabby face
looking in. His little nose was pressed against the

window. I couldn't hear him, but from the movement of his lips, I could see he was very unhappy. Poor Chester.

As for me, Mrs. Monroe spent the evening petting me and the family chatted with me all night long. And of course, I'd had my yummy steak dinner. So . . . it wasn't such a bad day after all.

Except that now my steak was all gone. Poor Harold.

Seven
A (NEW) FRIEND
IN NEED

In the days that followed, Chester's behavior was exemplary. He purred and he cooed and he cleaned his paws. And he rubbed up against everyone's legs to show what a good boy he was. I was getting worried. Chester acts that way only when he has something devious in the back of his mind. But I didn't know what it was. He had tried everything in the book to get rid of vampires, and all his efforts had failed. But I knew from the expression on his face that something was definitely up. Of course, I didn't know for certain because he had not spoken to me since the steak incident. I guess he realized that my heart just wasn't in the destruction of the bunny vampire.

In fact, I was beginning to like the little fellow.

The Monroes were relieved by Chester's improved behavior. They didn't know how to account for his strange doings but, to their credit, they were willing to let bygones be bygones. The only disturbing factor in all our lives was the reappearance of the white vegetables each morning in the kitchen. And yet, after a few days, even that stopped and life seemed to return to normal.

One evening, I dropped by Bunnicula's cage to chat. I'd found myself doing that more and more since Chester had stopped talking to me. Of course, Bunnicula didn't talk back, but he *was* a good listener. I'd begun to think of him as a friend—a strange one, granted, but one can't always choose one's friends. I was distressed this particular evening to see that he was dragging his ears, as it were. He looked tired and listless. I felt his nose and it seemed a little warmer than it should have been. I became alarmed.

I ran over to Toby who was doing a picture puzzle on the floor and began to bark—something I do only in cases of extreme emergency, since even I do not care for the sound.

"What's the matter, Harold?" Toby asked without moving. "Are there burglars?"

I ran to the cage and looked at Bunnicula. I looked back at Toby and whimpered. Toby just looked confused.

"Do you want to play with Bunnicula? Shall I take him out of the cage?'

"Woof," I responded, indicating, I hoped, that that was indeed what he should do.

"I'll ask Mom and Dad, Harold. You wait here." He was back in a minute, shaking his head. "I'm sorry, Harold, but Mom says you can't play with the rabbit. It causes too much commotion."

I looked down at the floor and whimpered again.

"Sorry, Harold, maybe later when we're all in here together."

I regarded Bunnicula whose eyes met mine. He gave a little shudder, and I felt like crying. My friend was sick, and I didn't know what to do. I wished I could tell Chester, but I knew it was no use. He was just too mad at me. I would have to sort this one out on my own.

That night, I couldn't sleep worrying about Bunnicula. I decided to go downstairs and check on his condition. What I saw when I entered the living room horrified me. Bunnicula was out of his cage on the floor, while Chester stood in front of him, a piece of garlic around his neck and his arms outstretched, blocking the kitchen door. Suddenly, it all fell into place. Chester was starving Bunnicula! Of course, *that's* why he seemed so listless, and that's why the vegetables had stopped turning white. Chester had made it impossible for Bunnicula to eat.

"Chester!" I cried.

Chester jumped a very high jump.

"What are you doing down here?" he spat at me as he landed.

"I know what you're doing, Chester, and the jig is up. That little bunny never hurt anybody. All he's doing is eating his own way. What do you care if he drains a few vegetables?"

"He's a vampire!" Chester snarled. "Today, vegetables. Tomorrow . . . the world!"

"I think perhaps you're overstating your case," I suggested cautiously.

"Go back to bed, Harold. This is larger than the two of us. It may seem harsh, but I'm only being cruel to be kind."

Who's he being kind to? I wondered, as I went back upstairs. The tomatoes and zucchinis of the world? Maybe a few cabbages? It just didn't make sense. But I could see I wasn't going to get anywhere with Chester tonight. Tomorrow, however, would be another story, and I was determined that, by hook or by crook, my friend Bunnicula would eat by sundown the next day.

Eight
DISASTER IN THE DINING ROOM

I realized that there was nothing I could do for Bunnicula during the day, since he was sleeping. But that gave me time to plan my strategy. At first, I thought I would bring food to his cage, but then it occurred to me that Chester must be taking everything away that was given to him. Pete and Toby usually left lettuce for Bunnicula during the day while he was sleeping, and Chester, ever watchful, probably nabbed it each evening just before the rabbit woke. No, there would have to be another way.

I thought and thought all afternoon, and I could

see that Chester had done a good job of isolating Bunnicula from his food. There was no way I could think of to overcome Chester's game plan. As evening drew closer and I grew more and more frantic, I stumbled into the dining room . . . and saw the answer to my problems sitting before me on the table. It was a big bowl of salad! All I had to do was get Bunnicula to the salad and let him get his fill before the family came in to eat. With that funny white dressing on it, they would never notice if a few vegetables were white.

I ran to the hallway to check the clock. Six fifteen. It would be fifteen minutes before the sun went down and Bunnicula woke up. I would then need at least five minutes to get him from his cage to the table and feed him. All I had to do was make sure no one came into the room until he had finished. I needed a good twenty minutes, at least.

I went back into the living room. Chester was asleep on his brown velvet chair, shedding in his sleep, still worn out from the previous night's activities. I checked upstairs. Toby was reading in his room, the last chapter of *Treasure Island*, I noted. Pete, who should have been doing his homework, was listening to records in his room.

I ran down to the kitchen.

"Hello, Harold," Mrs. Monroe said as I came through the door. "What's new?"

Other than a rabbit starving in the next room and an imminent attack on your salad bowl, nothing, I thought. I stood at her feet and panted. She scratched my head. This gave me a moment to check out how far she was in her cooking.

"Sorry, Harold," she said. "I have to baste this chicken." I noticed the oven timer still had thirty-five minutes to go. It'll be tight, I thought, but I can make it. Now, where is Mr. Monroe?

I went to the front door and whimpered loudly. Mrs. Monroe followed me.

"Are you waiting for Daddy, Harold? He'll be home soon."

Soon isn't good enough. *How* soon? I whimpered again.

"Patience, boy. He's late at a school meeting. He should be here any time."

She went back into the kitchen and I checked the clock. Six twenty-five. It was getting dark and Chester was still asleep. Time to swing into action.

Having watched Chester undo the lock on Bunnicula's cage and having participated in that unfortunate steak episode some days earlier, I knew I would have no problem getting Bunnicula out. I just had to be a little more careful where I positioned my head so that I wouldn't find myself in the humiliating predicament of getting stuck a second time. My timing was perfect. With Bunnicula swinging peacefully from my teeth, I made my way stealthily toward the dining room as the last rays of sunlight gave way to the dark of night. Once inside the dining room door, Bunnicula awakened in great bewilderment. It is not everyday, after all, that one finds oneself, upon awakening, hanging from the jaws of a fellow creature—even so caring and gentle a creature as myself.

Bunnicula opened his eyes wide and turned his face, as best he could, to me. I jumped up onto the nearest chair and placed the rabbit safely on the table's edge.

"Okay," I whispered, "there's your dinner. Go to it! Get your fill as fast as you can, poor bunny. I'll stand guard." I don't know that Bunnicula fully understood what was going on, but the sight of the vegetables piled high in the center of the table sent him scurrying in their direction. He was *very* hungry!

As luck would have it (and as I should have anticipated), Chester's sense of timing was as astute as my own. No sooner had Bunnicula reached the edge of the salad bowl than the door swung open and Chester bounded into the room. He surveyed the scene frantically. I was unable to act fast enough. Upon seeing Bunnicula about to enjoy his first bit of nourishment in days, Chester leaped across the table, seemingly without touching floor, chairs, or anything else between himself and our furry friend and landed directly on top of the bunny.

"Oh no, you don't!" he shrieked. Bunnicula, not sure what to do, jumped high in the air and landed, with a great scattering of greens, smack in the center of the salad bowl. Lettuce and tomatoes and carrots and cucumbers went flying all over the table and onto the floor. Chester flattened his ears, wiggled his rear end, and smiled in anticipation.

To cat observers, this is known as the "attack position."

"Run, Bunnicula!" I shouted. Bunnicula turned in my direction, as if to ask where.

"Anywhere!" I cried. "Just get out of his way!"

Chester sprang.

Bunnicula jumped.

And in the flash of a second, they had changed positions. Chester now found himself flat on his back (owing to the slipperiness of the salad dressing) in the bowl. And Bunnicula, too dazed to even think about food now, hovered quivering on the table.

Chester was having a great deal of difficulty getting back on his feet, but I knew it was only a matter of seconds before he'd attack again. And I knew also that Bunnicula was too petrified to do anything to save himself. So I did the only thing I could: I barked. Very loudly and very rapidly.

The whole family rushed through the doors. Mr. Monroe must have just come home because his coat was still on.

"Oh, no!" cried Mrs. Monroe. "That's it, Chester. This is Chester's last stand!"

Chester rolled his eyes heavenward and didn't even try to move.

"Mom," said Toby, tugging at his mother's arm, "look at Bunnicula. How did he get out of his cage? He looks scared."

"Of course, he's scared," Mrs. Monroe said. "We probably forgot to latch his cage and he got out. And I think Chester has been chasing him."

Toby put his face close to the rabbit. "Mom, doesn't Bunnicula look kinda sick?"

"We'd better take them all to the vet to see if any damage was done," she answered.

I started to whimper. No need for *me* to go to the vet.

Mr. Monroe patted my head. "We may as well take Harold along," he said. "He's probably due for his shots."

Mrs. Monroe carefully picked Chester out of the salad bowl and carried him by the scruff of the neck to the kitchen. "I'm going to give Chester a quick bath," she said to Mr. Monroe. "Why don't you put together a fresh salad? Toby, you and Peter put Bunnicula back in his cage and then clean up the table."

I didn't stick around for an assignment. This was not the time to be in the way.

And besides, I now had a whole evening and night ruined worrying about the next morning's visit to the vet. This little effort of mine, I thought, has been a disaster in more ways than one.

Nine
ALL'S WELL THAT
ENDS WELL . . . ALMOST

Looking back on that night, I remember thinking that this whole mess could never be resolved happily. What would become of Bunnicula, my new friend, who was suffering from starvation? And what of Chester, my old friend, who seemed to have flipped his lid and, if you'll pardon the expression, was in the doghouse with the Monroes? Of far greater concern at that time, of course, was my own future, for on that night all that consumed my thoughts was the fear of the next day's injections! It all seemed hopeless indeed.

But looking back on the next *day*, I can tell you

that happy endings are possible, even in situations as fraught with complications as this one was.

Early the next morning, we all piled into the car, some of us with greater reluctance than others, and trundled off to the vet. And by afternoon, we were on our way to solving our problems.

The vet worked everything out very nicely. He discovered that Bunnicula was suffering from extreme hunger. (*I* could have told him that.) Rather than jar his fragile stomach with solid foods, the doctor decided he should be put on a liquid diet until he got better. So Bunnicula was immediately given some carrot juice, which he drank eagerly. After he finished, he looked over at me with a great grin on his face and winked.

Chester was diagnosed as being emotionally overwrought. It was suggested that he start sessions with a cat psychiatrist to work out what the doctor called a case of sibling rivalry with Bunnicula. I asked Chester later what a sibling was, but he wasn't speaking to me. So I looked it up. It's like a brother or sister. And sibling rivalry means you are competing with your brother or sister for attention. I wasn't sure this was Chester's problem, but it sure explained a lot about Toby and Pete.

As for me . . . well, I came out the best. Dr. Wasserman was all set to give me my shots when the nurse came in with my card.

"Wait, doctor, this dog doesn't need his shots yet. It's too soon."

So I got a pat on the head and a doggie-pop instead.

These days, everything is back to normal in the Monroe household—almost. Bunnicula liked his liquid diet so much that the Monroes have kept him on it. And oddly enough, there have been no problems with vegetables mysteriously turning white since. Chester, of course, insists that this proves his theory.

"Obviously, Harold, the liquified vegetables take the place of the vegetable juices, so Bunnicula has no need to go roaming anymore."

"Then he's not a vampire," I said.

"Nonsense. He's a vampire all right. But he's a modern vampire. He gets his juices from a blender."

"Case closed, Sherlock?" I queried.

"Case closed."

"Oh, Chester . . ."

"Yes, Harold?"

"What are those two funny marks on your neck?"

Chester jumped and I laughed. "Very funny," he said as he began to bathe his tail, "very funny."

The Monroes never knew anything of Chester's theory. They changed markets and to this day believe they were the victims of a curious vegetable blight.

Bunnicula and I have become good friends. He still doesn't say anything, but he snuggles up next to me by the fireplace and we take long cozy snoozes together. One night, I sang him a lullaby in the obscure dialect of his homeland, and he slept very peacefully. It was that night that cemented our friendship.

Now—about Chester. I said that everything was back to normal—almost. Naturally, Chester is the "almost." He has been seeing his psychiatrist, Dr. Verrückt Katz, twice a week for some time now. He takes his therapy *very* seriously.

The other morning, I was trying to get a little sleep, when Chester came over and nudged me in the ribs.

"Harold, do you realize we've never really communicated? I mean *really* communicated?"

I opened one eye cautiously.

"And in order to communicate, Harold, you have to really be in touch with yourself. Are you in touch with yourself, Harold? Can you look yourself in the mirror and say, 'I know who I am. I am in touch with the me-ness that is me, and I can reach out to the you-ness that is you'?"

I closed my eye. I'm used to it by now. He talks like

that all the time. He no longer reads Edgar Allan Poe at night. And once he concluded that he had been right about Bunnicula, there has been no more talk about vampires. *The Mark of the Vampire* sits, its usefulness obsolete, on its shelf. Right now, he's reading *Finding Yourself by Screaming a Lot*, and the other night, when I heard the most awful noise coming from the basement, I didn't even bat an eyelid. I knew it was just Chester "finding himself," as he calls it. He explains to me that he's getting in touch with his kittenhood. And I've told him that's fine—just to let me know when he's going to do it, so I can be elsewhere. I've had enough trouble from Chester's adventures.

So that's my story. And the story of a mysterious stranger who no longer seems quite so mysterious and who is definitely no longer a stranger. I've presented the facts as clearly as I could, and I leave it to you, dear reader, to draw your own conclusions.

I must now bring this narrative to a close, since it is Friday night—Toby's night to stay up late and read—and I can hear the crinkling of cellophane. I can only hope it covers two chocolate cupcakes with cream filling.

BUNNICULA
THROUGH THE AGES

A Message from Max Brallier

"There was a flash of lightning, and in its glare I noticed that Mr. Monroe was carrying a little bundle—a bundle with tiny glistening eyes."

There it is. An all-time great sentence. The sentence that sucked me in, introduced me to the world of vampires, spooky stories, and the curious unknown. . . .

Bunnicula was unlike any book I'd read before. Things were happening that I simply did not understand. The editor's note? That blew my young mind! My eyes scanning the page: What is this? Is this story *real*? A manuscript? What is that? Does it mean that the *story behind the story* is real? I mean, grown-ups—people who make books—they can't just make up something like that, can they??

That questioning—that feeling of "What's real? What's not?" It surprised and confused me in a wonderful way. It was a page-turner before chapter one.

Bunnicula had me asking myself—what's really going on around me? I'd be reading one of Harold and Chester's brilliant back-and-forths, fascinated by their secret lives at the Monroe household. Then I'd pause, peeking over the top of the book, and I'd observe my dog Champ for a while. I'd wonder . . . What secret life was Champ living?

And even more! If dogs and cats could read and write, and bunnies could be vampires and hang out at movie theaters — then what other secrets were hiding in the ordinary of every day? I mean, here was a funny, imaginative, heart-pounding vampire story set entirely within the living room and kitchen of a very average family. No starships, no superheroes, no car chases. A living room, a kitchen, and an unexpected pet. That was it!

There were rabbits in my family's fenced-in backyard. I remember letting the dog out at night. Champ would hesitate at the door. I'd nudge him. Rabbits darting about in the moonlight. I nudged him further. I'd shut the door. There was barking. Just what was going on out there?

A few minutes would pass. Then pawing at the door. I'd open it — and Champ would rush in and take cover behind the sofa. What unknown world existed out there?

Bunnicula got my wheels turning. That flash of

lightning at the Monroe house? That was heavy voltage, an electrical dagger shot directly into my imagination.

To this day, *Bunnicula* is still unlike anything I've ever read. Scary, funny, strange, unexpected. I'm lucky to have read it as a child.

"There was a flash of lightning, and in its glare I noticed that Mr. Monroe was carrying a little bundle — a bundle with tiny glistening eyes."

That perfect sentence. The nervous energy in that brilliant opening scene. Flash! Glare! Glistening eyes! Do you hear the nervousness in Harold's voice? Oh boy, he's thinking, wondering, feeling — what strange wonder awaits?

MAX BRALLIER is the *New York Times* bestselling author of the Last Kids on Earth series, the Galactic Hot Dogs series, and Eerie Elementary series.

A Message from Holly Black

Bunnicula was my first vampire novel, sending me careening toward gothic fantasy and everything I love today. It's perfectly calibrated, keeping the reader off balance, not sure how frightening things are going to get.

There's such strangeness and specificity in the dry, white husks of vegetables. I vividly remember the frisson of fear I felt first reading about them—even though I am not a tomato, so I didn't have much to worry about. But there was also Chester, transformed from Harold's mild-mannered companion into a cat Van Helsing obsessed with taking down that small furry vampire—a vampire I was coming to like. And Bunnicula himself, silent in a book full of people and creatures that talk a lot, marking the rabbit as perhaps supernatural in nature after all.

And yet, for the genuinely scary parts, there is a remarkable gentleness to the story. It turns out that *strangeness* doesn't mean *wrongness*, and there's room in the world for loyal dogs, anxious cats, and vampire rabbits. Not to mention the people that live with them and try to do their best.

Recently, over several bedtimes, I read the first half of *Bunnicula* to my five-year-old son. Then I read the second half in a single breathless evening, because he wouldn't sleep until he heard the end.

HOLLY BLACK is the author of bestselling contemporary fantasy novels for kids and teens. Some of her best-known titles are the Spiderwick Chronicles series (co-created with Tony DiTerlizzi), the Modern Faerie Tales, *Doll Bones*, and *The Cruel Prince*. She has been a finalist for an Eisner Award and the recipient of the Andrew Norton Award, the Mythopoeic Award, and a Newbery Honor.

A Message from Dav Pilkey

I first read *Bunnicula* about thirty years ago, and was so inspired by the way it spoofed the horror and mystery genres with such humor and gentle affection. Thank you to Deborah and James for creating these wonderful stories and beloved, enduring characters.

To celebrate *Bunnicula*'s fortieth anniversary, I created my own cover image for the book. Here are Bunnicula, Harold, and Chester, à la Dav Pilkey!

DAV PILKEY is a Caldecott Honor Award–winning author and illustrator of many children's books. He is perhaps best known for his highly popular Captain Underpants and Dog Man series.

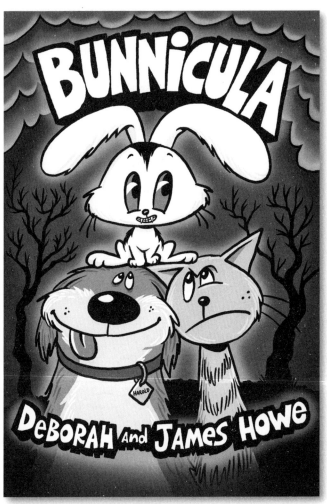

Bunnicula cover as imagined by Dav Pilkey

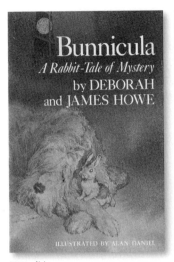

1979 edition.
Jacket artist: Alan Daniel

1980 Avon edition.
Jacket artist: Alan Daniel

1996 Aladdin edition.
Jacket artist: Alan Daniel

2006 Aladdin edition.
Jacket artist: C. F. Payne

"My first drawing in 1977 of Bunnicula even before the book idea was born."—James Howe

First drawing of Bunnicula in the original edition, 1979. Artist: Alan Daniel

Artist: Leslie H. Morrill

Nighty-Nightmare, 2010.
Jacket artist: C. F. Payne

Bunnicula Strikes Again!, 2010.
Jacket artist: C. F. Payne

Artist: Alan Daniel

Artist: Eric Fortune

Bunnicula Meets Edgar Allan Crow, 2010. Jacket artist C. F. Payne

Artist: Jeff Mack

Bunnicula and Friends:
The Vampire Bunny, 2004

BUNNICULA
FOREIGN LANGUAGE EDITONS

Artist: Francisco Nava Bouchain

Mexican edition, 2011

Artist: Marilyn Day

Italian edition, 1989

Deborah und James Howe

Kanicula

Eine rätselhafte
Kaninchengeschichte

Loewe

German edition, 1986.
Jacket artist: Werner Blaebst

Artist: Siglint Kessler

Deborah & James Howe

Kanicula

arsΞdition

A second German edition, 2001

UK edition, 2000.
Jacket artist: David Melling

Artist: Jean-Marie Renard

Deborah et James Howe

Cuniculicula

French edition, 1988

체스터가 내 쪽으로 고개를 돌리고는 선언하듯 말했다.
나는 우유 따위를 놓고 체스터와 다투고 싶
지 않았다. 토끼가 먹다 남긴 우유를 탐낼
만큼 치사한 내가 아니었다.
아이들이 나무 상자를 들고 나타났다.

Korean edition, 2004

Artist: Sungnam Kang

BUNNICULA
STAGE AND TELEVISION

The actors from the stage production of *Bunnicula*, from left to right: Tara Sytsma, Brian Panse, and Adam Carter (Credit: Farmers Alley Theatre, 2011)

Title image from the Warner Bros. Bunnicula television show on Boomerang

COMING SOON! Here's a sneak peek at our favorite vampire bunny as envisioned by Teemu Juhani in the graphic novel, coauthored by James Howe and Andrew Donkin.

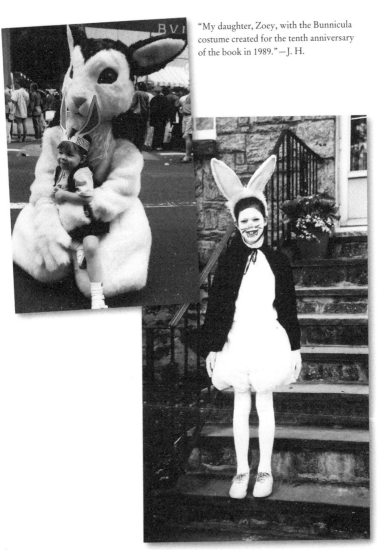

"My daughter, Zoey, with the Bunnicula costume created for the tenth anniversary of the book in 1989." —J. H.

"And here she is in 1995, dressed as Bunnicula for Halloween." —J. H.

READERS ARE ARTISTS TOO!

"I have read many books but none quite like _Bunnicula_."

This is a BUNNICULA

he or she is cute
I LOVE it

"Your writing style and techniques are interesting. I like them because they can suck your brain into a book."

Suck Suck

Suck

Bunnicula.

Don't ask why I have fangs

"THE BEST BOOK YOU EVER MADE WAS BUNNICULA. IF YOU GOT IT FROM YOUR LIFE, THAT WOULD BE SO COOL IF IT REALLY DID HAPPEN. I WOULD BE HORRIFIED BY THAT."

"Well, I guess this kinds of wraps it up.
Best wishes in your career as an author."

Photo copyright © Mark Davis

My career hasn't gone too badly in the forty years since *Bunnicula* was published. In addition to the six sequels and the spinoff series *Tales from the House of Bunnicula* and *Bunnicula and Friends*, I've written picture books; beginning reader series; young adult novels and short stories; and The Misfits series, which inspired the national antibullying initiative No Name-Calling Week. I hope my books have touched readers' lives with laughter and messages of hope, acceptance, respect, and celebrating one's uniqueness and creative spirit.

Enormous thanks to all the illustrators, writers, editors, agents, art directors and designers, animators, theater folks, librarians, teachers, trick-or-treaters, fan artists, and readers of all ages who have added so much of their creative spirit to the adventures of a vampire bunny and his creator.

To learn more about me and the story behind *Bunnicula*, please visit me at jameshowe.com.